Klaria's Battle

A Short Story

Heather Ewings

Quamby Press

Klaria's Battle

First Published in 'Cancer: Speculative Fiction Inspired by the Zodiac' (Deadset Press 2020), then in 'Wandering Stars: The Best of the Zodiac Series' (Deadset Press 2022)

Quamby Press

QuambyPress@outlook.com.au

A catalogue record for this book is available from the National Library of Australia

ISBN: 978-0-6488124-9-4

Cover image: Created in Canva

Klaria watched as Pedro heaved the canvas sack onto his back.

"Will ye come to town this time?" he asked, as he always did.

Klaria shook her head, as she always did. "My bleeding time has come."

She hadn't bled for years, but Pedro never seemed to notice she no longer hung her rags out to dry.

"No wee ones then?" Pedro's face fell.

"Sorry, love."

Pedro heaved the door of the hut open, and headed out into the cool spring day.

Klaria walked with him to the gate, watching until he disappeared out of sight down the slight incline of the meadow.

Klaria avoided town. It was too close to the ocean. She couldn't control herself near the sea, the urge to take to the waves too strong. She'd already scared herself once by nearly drowning.

It turned out she wanted life more than she wanted to go home.

She went back to the house. Pedro had packed the butter and eggs for the market, but he'd left her a fish caught fresh from the river this morning, still splashing in the bucket in the shade of the verandah. Klaria retrieved her basket and headed out to the garden. Fresh fish with salad greens would make a good dinner, and there'd be enough to leave in the meat safe for a cold breakfast the next morning.

The day passed slowly without company.

Klaria weeded the garden and gathered the eggs, the murmur of the chickens a comfort in the quiet. She swept out the single room of their small house, and spread the blankets across the line to beat out the dust. As the day drew to a close she returned to the house, to gut and cook the fish before dark.

For the most part, Klaria was pleased she and Pedro had not had children. She'd determined it, after all, drinking the tea recommended by the wise woman to stop babies coming, certain one day she'd find her shell and be gone, and not wanting to abandon an infant with a bereft father.

But days like this she wished she'd not been so certain of that future. It would've been nice to have a handful of children to fill the silence of the days when Pedro went to town.

She'd never found her shell. She'd scoured every inch of the property, outside and in, probing hollow tree trunks and abandoned animal burrows, searching in the wall cavities of the house and shed, and under all the loose floorboards.

Even under the floorboards securely nailed in place.

Wherever Pedro had hidden it, it wasn't here.

Dinner cooked, Klaria took her plate to the river's edge.

The moon would be full, and she wanted to sit where its light would fall upon her as it first rose.

She could escape the sea, it's pull not so strong here in the mountains. But she could not escape the moon, and the pull it exerted on her was far stronger.

Though she kept her gaze on her meal, her skin tingled when the moon first peered above the horizon. She held off from looking as long as she could, resisting the pull until she couldn't anymore and she gazed up at the full round moon, her vision blurring with tears.

Once she'd gathered with the other crab-folk, and they'd shed their shells and danced upon the sand, frolicking under the moon's rays.

Did they still do that, after all this time? Or had the human presence grown so large it was too dangerous?

She closed her eyes, two great drops rolling down her cheeks.

If only she could see her family again.

As if in answer there was a scuffling at the water's edge, and she opened her eyes as a large rock emerged from the river and scuttled up the bank.

Klaria stared. She knew what it must be, and yet it was too unlikely to be possible.

She'd never known a crab to come upstream. They didn't like the fresh water, weren't strong enough to swim against the downward current.

Still, two beady eyes emerged from one side of the rock, and it paused, scanning the surrounds, coming to rest on Klaria. It sidestepped towards her on the stony bank.

She held her breath. Sure enough, before it reached her, it propped itself up on it's four back legs, claws and two front legs waving in the air.

There was a distinct crack as the soft centre line of the undershell pulled apart, followed by much wriggling and squirming as a young, wet woman emerged from within.

At first she was small, child-sized to a human, but as she unfolded she stretched limbs and torso until she was almost as tall as Klaria.

She pulled herself to a sitting position, blinking a couple of times before her gaze landed on Klaria, and a beaming smile broke across her face.

"Aunt Klaria. I found you!"

Klaria's heart pounded, and she blinked several times herself, an attempt to clear her vision from this unexpected sight. Twenty-five years had passed since she'd seen another of her people.

Twenty-five years of settling into the certainty she'd never see them again.

"We need your help," the woman said.

"Who are you?"

"I'm Anabelle, Ninian's daughter."

"Ninian?" A lump formed in Klaria's throat at her younger sister's name. "Is she...?"

Anabelle raised her hands, palms facing Klaria. "She's fine. Scared, like we all are, but fine."

"Scared?" Klaria's fork clattered against the plate. "Why are you scared?"

"The townsfolk hunt us. We need you to come, to help us."

Klaria shook her head, and pushed herself to her feet.

"I can't help you." She took a step backwards. "There's nothing I can do."

"You know the human's ways," Anabelle insisted. "You've lived with them for two dozen cycles of the seasons. You can teach us what you know."

"I don't know anything. I've been living in the mountains, I only see my husband, and the few friends who drop in."

"He must talk," Anabelle said. "You would hear things."

"I don't have my shell." Klaria looked back at the house. Could she lock herself in?

She couldn't stand against the humans. She was weak, soft. Old. How could her people expect her to do anything?

6

Anabella shook her head. "You don't need your shell to teach us what you know."

Klaria imagined the pitying looks of her kin if she returned in her soft human form, and her chest constricted. "I can't come back without my shell!"

"Please, Aunt. You must come."

"I can't."

"They're killing us, Klaria. No one believes in the crab-folk anymore. They forget we are human inside, as they are, and they hunt us." She reached out to grab Klaria's hand, forcing Klaria to meet her gaze. "They *eat* us."

Klaria swallowed against the lurching in her stomach. "What about the other crab-women in town?"

Anabelle's eyes grew wide, and she shook her head. "They're all dead. They pined away for the sea. Died of heartbreak. You're the last still alive."

Klaria dropped back onto the bank, the breath knocked out of her.

"Seysill, Aine, Ena? Dead?"

Anabelle nodded. She squeezed Klaria's hand, and Klaria realised her niece was shivering.

She forced herself to stand. "Come inside. Let me find you a blanket."

Klaria lifted Anabelle's shell. It was large and cumbersome, awkward to wrap her arms around, and by the time they reached Pedro's hut her muscles ached.

Inside the fire burnt low, and Klaria added a few extra branches, pulling the blanket from her bed to wrap around Anabelle.

"I never knew it would be so cold in the mountains." Anabelle pulled the blanket tight around her shoulders. "I can barely feel my limbs."

Klaria reached out to rub some colour back into Anabelle's arms. "I'll get you some tea, and you can tell me what's happening."

Anabelle's story lasted well into the night.

The human population had tripled in the twenty-five years since Klaria was taken, their settlement spreading out along the shore, their buildings popping up in all the sheltered coves where the crab-folk had once gathered for their ceremonies. The humans hadn't liked to see the crab-folk dancing naked under the moon, and had chased them away, so now Klaria's people no longer gathered on the sandy shore, but on the rocky islands dotted off the coast, too sharp for the crab folk's soft human feet.

Where Klaria's childhood had been one of a truce between human and crab, Anabelle's early years involved a continuing cycle of loss. Family and friends were killed, at first while they danced upon the shore, and in later years in crab form, taken from the sea.

Klaria's stomach churned at the images Anabelle painted in her mind, her throat burning with anger, even as her cheeks were cooled with tears.

"You have to help us," Anabelle urged again. "You have to teach us what you know."

"I don't belong without my shell." Klaria shook her head.

Annabelle hesitated. "We know where your shell is."

"How? Why didn't you tell me this before."

"It's hidden in the inn where your husband sleeps when he visits town. My mother took human form, she—" Anabelle's eyes flicked away, but then her jaw set and she met Klaria's gaze again. "You should know. My mother seduced your husband. He told her how he loved you, as he made love to her, and when he left to go to the bathroom she searched the room. She said she felt it, as though you yourself were in the room with her. I didn't tell you because she couldn't find it. It could be locked away in the attic, or in the cellar. No one has access to those spaces except the innkeeper and his family."

Conflicting emotions swirled, so many Klaria didn't know which one to grab onto. Her sister seduced her husband, and he gave in to it, though he swore he'd never lay with another woman. Why did she hurt so much about the infidelity of a man she tolerated, a man who'd kidnapped her in the first place? She shook those feelings aside. All the more reason to escape.

If she had her shell she would be free. She could escape the man, and the mountain. She could return home.

"Can't she try again?" she asked Anabelle.

Anabelle shook her head. "It's too dangerous. We're not taking human form again, not until we know how to fight them."

A strange sense of calm swept through Klaria's body. Her shell had been found. With her shell, she could do anything. She could help Ninian, and Anabelle, and the rest of her people. She could lead them against the humans.

She looked at Anabelle. "Next full moon, Pedro will return to market. I will come with him. Gather everyone. I will find my shell, and I will return."

"You'll help us?" Anabella's face lit up.

Klaria nodded. "I'll help."

The month passed painfully.

Klaria wanted nothing more than to confront her husband with what she'd learnt, but what good would it do? He knew she never had visitors. He'd deny it, accuse her of paranoia. He might even refuse to allow her to join him the following moon.

Her days were spent arguing with herself; angry at her husband for laying with another woman, angry that the other woman was her sister, angry that Pedro had taken her shell from her in the first place.

But she was hurt too, and that baffled her the most. He was a foolish human who couldn't get a wife by any other means, and yet she'd grown fond of him, of all the thoughtful little things he did to make her life as comfortable as possible.

Everything except grant my freedom.

12

Finally the time came. Pedro heaved the sack up onto his back, and Klaria waited for him to invite her along.

He approached her, kissed her forehead, and turned to leave.

"I, uh—" Klaria began.

"Yes?" He turned. "Is everything all right?"

Klaria rung her hands together. "I thought I might come with you, this time."

"You're not bleeding?"

Klaria shook her head. "Not today."

His eyes lit up. "Do you think there's a wee one on the way?"

Klaria licked her lips. Could she lie to him? She shook her head.

"It's too early to tell."

He nodded, but still his eyes shone in a way they hadn't for years.

"A son," he said. "To carry my name." He glanced at her. "And now your barrenness has lifted, he will soon be followed by a daughter to carry yours."

He beamed, and Klaria forced a smile. Better to allow their last days together to be happy ones.

Pedro was not often talkative, but now his spirits were up he filled the walk to town dreaming about the future, about the rooms he would build onto the house, about how he would teach his child to fish, and garden, and hunt.

"They'll be self-sufficient like we are," he announced. "Not like the young folk in town, growing up with no idea how to care for themselves, nor what their place is in the world. That's what's causing all the problems in the world today. One day it'll all crash down around them, and then where will they be? Starving, that's where." He shook his head. "I'll have no children of mine in that position."

Klaria listened, nodding whenever he looked her way, making small noises of agreeance now and again, so he felt she was listening.

They reached town by nightfall, the moon fat and round on the horizon.

It called to her, as it always did, but now something else pulled her, too. Lapping at the edges of her senses were rivulets of energy, drawing her home.

A strange longing overpowered her as they approached the inn, a pull that led her feet to the very place Pedro wanted to go.

The inn keeper gave her a strange look, but Pedro introduced her as his wife, and the innkeeper nodded.

It was all Klaria could do not to run to the room, and once in the room, not to seek out the hiding place where he'd hidden her shell.

Pedro set their bags down and knelt before the empty fire place, scrunching up bits of bark into a ball and placing it in the grate.

"What can I do?" Klaria asked, her skin buzzing.

"Help me with the fire." He gestured to the basket of kindling. "It gets cold here at night. The chill wind whips off the water and sneaks in through the gaps, and these days my bones ache when it's too cold."

Klaria did as he asked.

Once the fire was burning, she asked if she might go for a walk.

He grunted a reply, that she could do whatever she wanted.

Outside the night air felt crisp against her face. Klaria pulled her shawl tighter around her shoulders, and followed the narrow path to the shore.

With every step she fought the pull to turn back, to retrieve her shell. There was no point. She couldn't do it now, not with Pedro there.

She'd hoped to find the beach empty at this time of night, but there were people scattered all along the shore. Fishermen strode into the sea with long nets, muttering to each other. Further along a man paced, and when Klaria drew closer she saw he was holding a baby, patting it's back in time with his steps.

He glanced at Klaria as she walked past, his eyes drawn.

She offered him a weak smile.

"Do you know how to get a baby to sleep?" he asked.

Klaria shook her head and kept walking.

A young couple strolled hand-in-hand along the sea's edge, the waves lapping at their ankles. And further, around a curve in the coast, a group of young men loitered on the sand, the scent of ale carried on the breeze.

Was there nowhere where the crab-folk could safely come ashore?

Klaria came to a stand of rocks, jutting out into the sea. The points were hard on her feet, but she followed them as far out as she could, until the sea splashed around her ankles and sent her feet slipping.

She flung out her arms, her heart racing as she steadied herself. It would do no good to fall into the water in her heavy skirts. Pedro would be angry, *if* she managed to pull herself out of the sea, and she couldn't help her people if she were dead.

She took a few steps back, and sat down.

"Ninian," she called, her voice soft. "Ninian!"

It would take time for her call to be heard under the waves, time she wasn't sure she had.

Would Pedro be asleep? Or was he wondering where his wife was, and what she was up to?

Could he be suspicious of her sudden desire to join him in town, or did he truly believe she carried his child, that the connection would be enough to make her stay?

The moon was high in the sky now. The wash of the waves made Klaria want to dance, but if she did the human-folk would know by her movement she was truly crab and that would only be trouble.

She wondered how her family coped below the waves, feeling the moon's presence, and yet unable to come to the shore.

The waves washed again, in and out. Was no one coming? She was about to stand when a crab scuttled up the rock and peered at her.

"Ninian?"

The eyes swayed ever so slightly, and Klaria felt a surge of panic that she had forgotten what her sister looked like.

"Is that you?"

One claw raised, and snapped. Yes.

"Can you not change, for a moment?"

Two claws raised and snapped together. No.

Klaria glanced around, realising the group of young men on the beach were on their feet, watching her.

"I know where my shell is," Klaria said. "I'll find a way to get it. When I do, I'll be back."

Ninian's claws clacked together, two, three, four times, in quick succession.

Klaria nodded.

"I'll be as quick as I can."

Back at the room, Pedro snored soundly. Klaria took a moment to peer under the bed, but the fire was nothing more than hot coals, and gave little light. She pressed her fingertips against the floorboards, feeling for gaps or loose, wobbly boards.

Nothing.

Then she realised that the nails had been removed from the board directly beneath the bed's leg

Her breath caught.

It must be there.

She couldn't grab her shell now, but if she waited until Pedro went to market the next morning...

She undressed, and climbed into bed. Pedro snorted and rolled over, a heavy arm crossing her shoulders. She forced her breathing into a slow even rhythm.

Morning couldn't come fast enough.

Klaria tossed and turned, disturbing Pedro enough that he snapped at her in the early hours of the morning, taking most of the blanket with him as he rolled away, the bed rocking from his movement.

She waited until his snores started up again, and then sidled up close, careful to lay extra still under the tiny portion of blanket available to her.

She didn't sleep.

When Pedro woke she slowed her breathing, listening as he climbed out of bed and pulled on his shirt and trousers.

There was silence for a moment, and then his lips pressed against her forehead, and she heard him add another log to the fire, the door clicking as he left the room.

Klaria waited a moment longer. When there was no other movement she opened her eyes.

The room was empty.

She took a deep breath.

After all this time. If only she'd accompanied Pedro on his trips to market from the beginning! But she'd been so scared after that first time, when she'd nearly drowned trying to return to her home. When she couldn't find her shell at his home, she'd assumed he'd hidden it somewhere along the path to town, or else higher in the mountains. The task of searching such an area had seemed impossible, and she'd given up, too easily. She'd never imagined for a moment he'd leave it behind in the town itself.

She shook her head, and slid out of bed.

The bed was made of solid wood, bulky and heavy. Klaria pushed against it, satisfied to feel it shift under her effort. But then it bumped against something and wouldn't budge any further.

She knelt by the bed to try to manoeuvre the floorboard, but the bed hadn't moved far enough to move it, so she lifted the bed again, her muscles straining against the effort. Something stopped the bed from moving.

21

She went around to the other side of the bed.

There was a nail jutting from the floor, preventing the leg on this side from sliding any further.

Klaria bit her lip. She didn't have any tools to remove the nail, so instead she lifted the bed, heaving it towards her.

Sweat dripped into her eye, stinging. The fire flared, and she wished Pedro hadn't bothered to stoke it before he left.

Finally the bed slid easily, and Klaria slipped, dropping the bed with a thud.

She froze, straining her ears, but couldn't hear anything over the pounding of her heart.

When there was no movement in the hallway, she took a drink of water from the jug on the mantlepiece, forcing her breath to slow enough so she could hear over the beating of her heart.

All still quiet, she knelt by the odd floorboard. She could *feel* her shell through the thin strip of wood, reaching out to her just as much as she reached out to it.

There was no indent to fit her finger, but Klaria pushed on one end and the whole board tipped upwards.

A waft of salty sea air reached her nose, and then Klaria saw it, the brilliant blue of her shell, visible under years of dust. She set the floorboard to one side and reached in, a current of energy zapping along her fingertips as she touched the hard surface, tears rolling down her face, creating shiny trails on the shell where they washed away the dust.

She had to press the under side of the shell up into the indentation of the back to get it up through the narrow gap, the legs and claws clattering against the wood as they came through.

"I never thought I'd find you again," Klaria whispered, her breath catching at just how her shell gleamed even after all this time.

"What have you done?"

The voice boomed. Klaria turned as Pedro crossed the room, his face red, the veins in his neck bulging. She hugged the shell as she stood, stepping away from Pedro's anger.

"I—"

He crossed the room in two strides, grabbing the legs of her shell and ripping it from her hands.

"No!" Her voice was a howl. "Please."

"I've kept you safe, all this time." He waved her shell in the air. "You're going to leave? Now you're with child? Is that why you stayed so long?"

It took Klaria a moment to understand what he was talking about.

She clenched her fists.

"There is no child. There's been no bleeding for years, though you don't care enough to notice. I never stayed because I wanted to, I stayed because I had no choice." Her eyes darted from Pedro's face to her precious shell.

"But now..." She lunged for her shell, and in the same movement he swung it back, flinging it into the fire.

Everything moved in slow motion.

Klaria's fingertips brushed a claw as she fell through the air, pain jolting up her body as her knees crashed against the floor.

The shell spun, round, and again, and once more, before it landed with a puff of ash and smoke among the flames.

Neither Pedro or Klaria moved for a moment, and then pain shot up Klaria's right side and across her back as flames licked the underside of the shell.

"No!"

She pulled at her clothes a moment too long before she realised it wasn't the fabric that was burning.

"Save it. Save it!" She screamed at Pedro, who watched her wide eyed as she clawed at the pain now shooting across her face.

Finally he jerked into action, grabbing the poker to knock the blackened shell from the fire.

Klaria collapsed on the floor, her chest heaving.

"Love. I'm sorry. I didn't know." He was by her side in an instant, brushing hair from her face. "I didn't realise."

He pulled on her shoulder. Klaria tried to push his hand away, but he was too strong and he rolled her over.

His hand covered his mouth as he recoiled. "Oh, Love. What have I done?"

Klaria brought her hands to her face. She flinched as her fingers brushed her cheek, the pain still raw though the burning sensation had stopped.

When she gingerly touched her cheek again there were bumps and valleys, her skin puckered from the heat.

Tears filled her eyes, and she scrambled for her shell.

Pedro just watched as she picked it up, examining the charred crack that almost split the shell in two, the crisp underside that had been soft and pliable moments before.

"What have you done?" she asked him, tearing off her blouse to swing the shell up and over her shoulders.

She waited for the sense of suction, pulling her back into her true form, but the hard edges of the shell just poked into her skin.

"What have you done!" She wailed, trying to push herself inside the shell that wouldn't take her.

"What have you done?" She sank to the floor.

Her stomach churned, and she sucked in deep breaths of air that never seemed to reach her lungs.

"Love. I'm sorry. I didn't know." Pedro's gaze was pitiful.

Rage burned in the pit of her stomach and she pushed herself to her feet.

"You ruined me." She waved her shell at him. "You ruined my life. But I won't let you and yours ruin the lives of my people."

Pedro flinched, and Klaria stormed out, ignoring the stares of those she passed, peering out of their rooms. She strode to the beach, grabbing the first dinghy she could find. Throwing her damaged shell inside, she pushed it out into the waves.

Somewhere there must be a quiet space for the crab-folk to come ashore.

She just had to find it.

Klaria rowed until her arms shook under the strain, but everywhere there were signs of human habitation. Small coves were watched by lonely cottages, while on the shores of larger bays houses snuggled together as though for safety.

How was she supposed to protect her people from humans, when the creatures were everywhere?

The oars slipped from her hands, and Klaria watched them float away before laying down in the boat, her gaze on the clouds above.

She was not human. But now, she was also not crab.

The sun beat down on her from above, the heat searing her skin. She welcomed the pain, which matched the intensity in her chest, the burning in her lungs as she sucked in each breath, and tearing in her heart as Pedro's act replayed again and again in her mind.

Who knew her shell could be so badly damaged, and she could still live?

She dozed, waking as her boat bumped against something solid.

The sun was even higher in the sky, her skin red from its rays. Her throat hurt, and her lips were dry.

She pushed herself up, blinking at her surroundings.

Across the waves she could see the coast, houses dotted all the way along. When she turned, she found herself at a rocky island, barely more than two dozen steps across. She climbed out on unsteady feet, leaving the boat to the current.

Movement in her periphery caused her to turn.

A crab scuttled along the shore towards her, then another lifted it's beady eyes above the water, and it too emerged from the shallows. Soon she was surrounded.

"I failed," she told her family, showing them her damaged shell. "I can't help you."

A crab came close, grabbed the edge of her trousers with a claw, and pulled.

"I'm coming."

The crab released her, and scuttled towards the centre of the island, where the rocks were higher. Here Klaria found a rock pool, sea-water and rain-water mixing and she lowered her mouth to drink great soothing gulps.

When she was done she sat in the semi-shade provided by the rocks, holding tight to her shell.

All around, more crabs gathered.

Klaria must have dozed again, for she woke to the sound of a hundred shells cracking.

All around her the crab-folk were emerging. They came to her, and held her in their arms, and they cried together for the loss of her shell, and for the loss of their people, and for the loss of their cove.

"Tell us about the humans." Ninian said. "Tell us how we can defeat them."

"We cannot defeat them in human form," Klaria said. "We're too vulnerable. Our shells are our armour. But we can only defeat them if we all stand up to them. If we all storm the beach together they will be afraid, and they will flee, and then we'll get our cove back."

"Can you lead us?"

Klaria shook her head.

"My shell is broken beyond repair. I can't help anyone now."

An older woman stepped forward, and took hold of Klaria's shell.

"You would not still live if your shell was destroyed beyond repair," she said. "There are salves that can help a damaged shell." She turned Klaria's shell over in her hands. "I don't know how much we can help this one, but we can try."

She called over several of the younger women who retrieved their shells and, in crab form, disappeared into the sea.

"While Isla seeks to mend your shell, we must make plans," Ninian said. "You must tell us the weapons of the humans."

Klaria nodded, and thought of all the things that could be used as weapons. Of what she would use for a weapon, if she needed to. "They have bows and arrows, and spears for hunting fish, and nets to tangle their prey. If they come from their gardens they have forks and spades and hoes and axes. There are rolling pins, and heavy pans."

Anabelle shook her head. "What are all those things? What do you mean?"

Klaria explained in detail, the size and shape and sharpness or bluntness of the item. "Their heavy items could crack shells, but their sharp items may be deflected."

She looked around at the group around her.

"They are superstitious. If we gathered the crab-folk from all along the coast and swarmed the beach together we might scare them so that they ran at first sight and we did not have to fight."

The other crab-folk nodded, taking in Klaria's words.

"Then that is what we will do." Ninian turned to face the gathered crowd. "We will wait until Isla returns with her salve, and we will see if Klaria can be healed. And then we will reclaim our home!"

A cheer went up through the crab-folk.

That night Klaria ate the food of her childhood; limpets, and seaweed, and tiny shrimp. The salty-freshness brought tears to her eyes, as she realised how many years had passed since last she'd eaten food that she truly loved.

They sat on their shells and spoke of the passing years, and their different experiences, and in the early light of dawn Isla and her assistants returned. Isla held a clam shell, shut fast, and passed this to Ninian before she removed her shell.

In human form she turned to Klaria. "I do not know how well this will work. I've never seen a shell so badly burnt, where the wearer was still alive. It may be too far gone."

Klaria closed her eyes as Isla smoothed the salve over the shell first, and then over Klaria's burns.

"Face the moon before it sets completely," Isla instructed, and Klaria did so, aware of the growing light behind her as the dark ahead began to fade.

Her burns tingled, the puckered skin on her face stinging as the salve did its work.

She didn't dare look at her shell.

As the moon dropped below the horizon, Isla massaged Klaria's back.

"Shall we try it now?"

Klaria swallowed the lump in her throat, trying to ignore the swirling in her stomach. She held her shell. The top side was still cracked, the softer underside still hard.

"Will it work? Would it be better to give it longer?"

"If it does not work now, it will never work."

Klaria nodded, and squeezed her eyes shut tight as Isla lifted the shell and placed it across Klaria's shoulders.

Klaria held her breath.

Across her back the tiny tendrils of her human body reached out, connecting with the tendrils from her shell.

Her eyes flew open.

"It's working," she whispered.

But then it stopped.

The shell fused with Klaria's shoulders, but Klaria's body was not pulled inside.

Klaria's heart pounded as she tried to fold herself into her shell, tried to pull the now-hardened underside of the shell around her chest, but nothing took hold.

"Argh!" She spun around, screaming her frustration at the sky. "I'm ruined."

She felt a light touch through her shell, and glanced to see Isla examining her.

"You're not ruined," Isla said. "You're merging just isn't complete."

Isla bent down to tear long strands of seaweed from the rocks at their feet, and strapped the now-brittle under-shell together across Klaria's chest.

"Let's see," she said, lifting her own shell. "Come into the water with me. Let's see if you can breathe and swim. You might still be able to lead us. You might be stronger than you were before."

Klaria doubted it, but still she followed Isla's crab form into the water, her shell an extra weight on her shoulders, her six crab legs waving uselessly.

Her heart sank as the water rose about her, covering her knees, her thighs, her hips. How could she possibly be of any use to anyone like this?

She hoped for nothing more but that the weight of her shell would send her to the bottom, where she could leave the pain of this life behind.

But as the water covered her shoulders Klaria felt lifted by sea. She took a deep breath, closed her eyes, and submerged herself beneath the surface.

Strange grey swirls swam before her eyes, and it took her a moment to work out that she was seeing through her crab eyes. She released the breath in her lungs, only to find her lungs had merged into gills and she could breathe.

Isla's claws clattered together in front of Klaria's face, expressing joy in Klaria's strange new form.

All of a sudden, the clicking noises around her became clear as speech, and Klaria understood that all her people offered support and joy that she was with them again.

"We will face the humans tonight," Isla said. "We will storm our cove, and reclaim it for our people."

"I am deformed." Klaria said.

"You are you, and you are back, and together we are stronger."

Klaria forced a smile, though inside her stomach churned. Her people needed her. They could not continue to live as they were. Perhaps feigning confidence would be enough?

The crab folk gathered in the deep of the cove, and spent the day feasting on clams and snails and algae. Above the waves the afternoon wore on, as below they told stories of the times when they were free to shed their shells and take human-form, and sing and dance in ways they could not under the sea.

As the light filtering through the water faded, the crab-folk began their scuttle over the sea bed, determination buoying their spirits.

By the time they reached the shallows, the moon was visible just above the horizon.

Klaria, Isla, and Ninian approached the surface, their crab-eyes extended above the water.

As Klaria had seen on her first night in the town, fishermen gathered along the shore, great nets spread out. People walked the shoreline, couples, friendship groups, singles.

Klaria held her breath. Was Pedro there, somewhere? Was he searching for her, or had he returned to their empty mountain home? Did he feel as lost as she had, when he first took her shell and hid it away?

All around her the crabs shells clattered together as they tried to settle. Her heart seemed to beat just as loudly. Couldn't the humans hear it?

Klaria saw no indication from those on the shore.

She took a deep breath, exhaling forcefully as though doing so could expel the tiny fish darting about in her stomach, and clicked her claws twice in the sign to charge.

All around her, crabs surged up the beach.

Klaria watched as the humans turned, shouted and stared.

They didn't run.

Why didn't they run?

"Fresh crab tonight, fellas!" one fisherman called, gathering one end of his large net. The others followed suit, and soon nets stretched across the length of the beach, several men on each end as they walked back towards the water, scooping up crabs in their wake who ended up upside down and sideways as the nets caught them up and tumbled them over each other.

"No." Klaria stood, but in the chaos the men paid no attention, and they came around behind and then pulled on the net, scooping up all the crab-folk and dragging them up the shore.

Klaria was knocked over, face down in the sand, her arms and legs tangled up the net, almost smothered by crab-folk.

That's when the killing started.

Thuds and thwacks from the human's clubs filled the air. The cracks and crunching of shell, and the cries of her people, mingled with the excitement of the humans at such a feast.

"No!" Klaria twisted her head, spitting out sand. "Help."

"Wait." A voice called in the darkness. "There's a woman in there."

"I'll save her."

Men walked across the net, their heavy boots cracking open the shells of those they stepped on.

Klaria's stomach lurched at the sound.

"Stop, please."

The net around her was cut away, the crabs picked up and thrown.

Klaria felt a hand on her own shell, felt it being lifted, then dropped.

"The crab's trying to eat her!"

From the corner of her eye Klaria saw the man lift his club.

"No, please."

Down it came, pain shooting down her spine as she screamed out for help.

"We'll get it off you, don't worry."

Another thwack across her shoulders. Klaria bit her tongue, a sharp tang filling her mouth.

"Stop." Klaria's cry was strangled.

"Help me with this, will you?"

Four hands this time, on either edge of her shell.

She was lifted for the briefest time, and then dropped again, her head thumping on the hard sand beneath her.

"What the—"

"What is she?"

This time a hand came under Klaria's shell, and pulled her over onto her back.

Two faces looked at her in disgust.

"She's one of those crab people. From the stories." A young man spoke, his eyes wide.

"Don't be stupid." His companion laughed. "That's just a myth."

"Look at her." An older man stepped into Klaria's view, nudging her shell with his foot. "She's a crab person all right."

The second young man grimaced. "Monster!" he shouted, raising his club in the air.

"Wait!" Another voice, a familiar voice, and as Klaria blinked in a losing battle for her vision, Pedro's face swam into view.

"I'm sorry, love," he said. "I'm so sorry." He turned to the men surrounding him. "Who're the monsters here? The ones being killed, or the ones doing the killing?"

The young man who'd recognised her as crab-folk dropped his club.

"We've taken so much from them," Pedro continued. "We need to give back."

He turned back to Klaria. "I'm so sorry, Love" he repeated. "I never wanted to hurt you. I didn't mean to steal you from your family, your home. I just wanted to be with you."

His words faded as the world went black.

When Klaria woke all was quiet.

She was still on the beach, but had been moved up to where the sand was softer. Towards the sea she could see movement, human figures lifting things from the sand and carrying them down to the ocean.

Crabs.

Humans were carrying crabs, which hung limply in their arms.

She'd failed.

She'd brought destruction on her people, not salvation. Now they not only had no cove in which to safely change form, their entire community had been slaughtered.

"You're awake."

Klaria glanced up to see Anabelle watching over her.

"Anabelle. You're alive?"

Anabelle smiled. "Of course I'm alive. And Ninian, and Isla. They're down there with the others, helping to heal the wounds of the injured."

"The injured?" Klaria frowned, and glanced back across the beach.

Now she realised that none of the human figures wore any clothing, that they all held the crumpled crabs carefully as they carried them to the sea.

To the sea, Klaria realised. Not to their village, to a cooking pot or fire.

These weren't humans, they were crab-folk in human form.

"What happened?" She glanced back at Anabelle.

"You don't remember?"

Klaria shook her head.

"Your husband came. He made them stop. He said they must give us back this cove, that no human must step foot here again. Look." Anabelle pointed up to the hilltops all around, where Klaria could see men, human men, hammering at stakes in the ground. "They're fencing the area off, so that no humans will come again. You won us the battle, Klaria. You returned to us our cove."

Klaria couldn't believe it.

"Is it real?"

Isla approached.

"The sea is healing our injuries," she said. "And the humans have left. It's real."

Klaria pushed herself to a sitting position, suddenly aware her shell was no longer attached to her shoulders.

"The sea can't heal me," she said.

Isla shook her head.

"No. But we can visit you now, as we couldn't before, and you can wear your shell and visit with us under the waves, in your new form."

Klaria swallowed back the lump in her throat. She could not return home, not properly, but she was alive, and she was back with her people.

As the days passed the crab-folk brought driftwood and built Klaria a home on the shoreline. She kept her shell on the wall above the mantle, taking it down whenever she needed to be submerged under the waves, and when the moon was full joined her people in human form to dance and sing and celebrate as they always had.

And the humans kept their word, and the crab-folk never had to fear them again.

Thank you!

Thank you so much for reading my folk tale. Klaria's Battle was born out of a call for speculative fiction based around the zodiac – as a Cancerian myself, I wanted to write a story around Cancer the Crab. At the time, I hadn't long published 'What the Tide Brings' and 'Maggie and the Selkie' so my head was still very much stuck in the selkie folklore space, and so 'Klaria's Battle' was born. It was first published in 'Cancer: Speculative Fiction Inspired by the Zodiac' (published by Deadset Press), and then later selected to be part of 'Wandering Stars: The Best of The Zodiac Series', so check out the other stories in those anthologies (and the rest of the Zodiac series) if you get the chance!

And if you enjoyed this story, please consider leaving a review on Goodreads, or on the site where you bought it. Reviews are a great way for me to see what you liked, and what I should write more of! And if you do, let me know! I'd love to share it as a thank you for helping me reach new readers. ❤

And if you'd like to be kept up-to-date on my latest news head over to my website at https://heatherewings.com.au and sign up to my newsletter!

About the Author

Heather Ewings is an Australian author of speculative fiction, with a MA in History and an urge to save the world by looking at what knowledge we've lost/forgotten/ignored from the past. Her debut novella 'What the Tide Brings' was first printed for inclusion in The People's Library Project in Sep 2018, and then published in the midst of lockdown in 2020, alongside the prequel short story 'Maggie and the Selkie'. In 2022 she received an Honorable Mention in the Stillhouse Press Novella Competition for 'Fixing Kendra', a novella exploring the consequences of Time Travel. Her short stories have been published all over the web, the shortest of which are collected in 'Not Entirely Human And Other Stories'.

Heather lives among gum trees and wattles, where she balances her time home schooling her youngest child, making beeswax candles, and attempting to grow some veggies among the weeds.

Visit https://heatherewings.com.au to learn more about Heather's work.